⊷ Book Six ⊷

EPOS
THE WINGED FLAME

⤙ Book Six ⤚

Epos
The Winged Flame

Adam Blade
illustrated by Ezra Tucker

SCHOLASTIC INC.

New York Toronto London Auckland Sydney
Mexico City New Delhi Hong Kong Buenos Aires

With special thanks to Stephen Cole
To Matthew Egerton

No part of this work may be reproduced, stored in a retrieval system, or transmitted in any form or by any means, electronic, mechanical, photocopying, recording, or otherwise, without written permission of the publisher. For information regarding permission, write to Working Partners Ltd., Stanley House, St Chad's Place, London, WC1X 9HH, United Kingdom.

ISBN-13: 978-0-439-02458-7
ISBN-10: 0-439-02458-7

Beast Quest series created by Working Partners Ltd, London.
BEAST QUEST is a trademark of Working Partners Ltd.

Published by Scholastic Inc., 557 Broadway, New York, NY 10012, by arrangement with Working Partners Ltd.

SCHOLASTIC, LITTLE APPLE, and associated logos are trademarks and/or registered trademarks of Scholastic Inc.

12 11 10 9 8 7 6 5 4   8 9 10 11 12 13/0

Designed by Tim Hall
Printed in the U.S.A.
First printing, March 2008

BEAST QUEST

BEASTQUEST

→ BOOK SIX ←

EPOS
THE WINGED FLAME

Reader,

Welcome to Avantia. I am Aduro — a good wizard residing in the palace of King Hugo. You join us at a difficult time. Let me explain. . . .

It is laid down in the Ancient Scripts that the peaceful kingdom of Avantia would one day be plunged into danger by the evil wizard, Malvel.

That time has come.

Under Malvel's evil spell, six Beasts — fire dragon, sea serpent, mountain giant, night horse, ice beast, and winged flame — run wild and destroy the land they once protected.

The kingdom is in great danger.

The Scripts also predict an unlikely hero. They say that a young boy shall take up the Quest to free the beasts and save the kingdom.

We pray this young boy will take up the Quest. Will you join us as we wait and watch?

Avantia salutes you,
Aduro

PROLOGUE

I'M LOST, THOUGHT OWEN. THE TUNNEL ended in yet another dark cave. Panic rose in the boy's throat as he tried to retrace his steps. But he knew it was hopeless. Although he had left chalk markings on the rock walls, it was too dark to see them.

Only a while ago, Owen had been playing outside the caves on the north side of the village. Then he had heard noises coming from inside the caves. Scraping, scrabbling noises. People hardly ever entered the caves, as they were unsafe and stretched for miles underground. Rockfalls were common, too. But he couldn't just ignore whatever was in there.

An animal must have wandered in and got lost, he'd told himself. *It won't take long to help the poor thing back out.*

He had tried to follow the scrabbling sounds he had heard — and now he was hopelessly lost. He stood helpless in the cold blackness.

"Is anyone there?" he called. His voice echoed eerily back at him. These caves took the slightest sound and twisted it, making it seem as though it came from one direction when it came from another.

He felt ahead and his fingers brushed against pitted rock — then nothing. Stepping forward, Owen realized he'd found the mouth of a new cave. A little way in, there was a faint light. He looked up and saw a chink of gray sky in the rock, high above.

Then his foot scraped against something on the floor. It was a piece of scorched armor. Where had this come from? And what had happened to the knight who had worn it? It looked like a bevor — which knights used to protect the chin and lower face — only smaller.

Suddenly, a terrifying screech sliced through the air. Owen yelled out in terror, staring around wildly.

A dark shape detached itself from the shadows and towered over him. In horror, Owen realized it was a giant bird!

Its huge, sail-like wings unfurled. They were covered in short, dark-gold feathers. Its beak was as long and sharp as a sword. Two fierce eyes fixed on Owen, blazing like irons in a blacksmith's fire. The creature's huge talons were scratching on the rock, tearing it up. Heart pounding, Owen realized that this was the sound he had heard. Here was the animal he had hoped to rescue. . . . Now he needed rescuing — and fast!

The creature lurched toward him — and then its massive, feathered bulk burst into flame! Owen hurled himself to the ground as the Beast launched into the air, its great, fiery wings beating wildly as it flew straight at him.

→ CHAPTER ONE ←

THE FIERY THREAT

"**W**E MUST BE NEARLY THROUGH THE FOREST now," Tom called to his friend Elenna, who was walking behind him. He drew his sword and hacked at the thorny thicket barring his way. The light was thin, the gray sky barely visible through the heavy branches overhead.

"I hope so," Elenna called back. She was leading Storm, Tom's sturdy black stallion. She stopped for a moment, leaning against the horse for support. "I sure could use a good rest!"

They had been traveling for nearly two weeks and were both exhausted. It had been a long Quest, but they were almost done. There was just one more Beast to defeat before they could return home.

"I'm tired, too," Tom said solemnly. "But we must keep going — the kingdom needs us."

"Not many people would be in such a rush to battle Epos the Winged Flame!" said Elenna, a weary smile spreading on her face.

Tom smiled back, but didn't slow down. With a swell of determination, he raised his sword and swiped fiercely at the undergrowth. He was on a vital quest for King Hugo and he couldn't give up now, with the end in sight.

His mission was to save the kingdom from the Beasts — creatures of legend placed under an evil spell by the Dark Wizard Malvel. Tom used to think the Beasts were just fairy tales. But now he knew there was nothing make-believe about them.

Elenna and her wolf Silver had joined Tom and Storm on the Quest, and together they had risked their lives trying to set the Beasts free from Malvel's curse. They had already stood up to a one-eyed giant and a slithering sea serpent. They had tamed a night horse, a fire dragon, and a terrifying ice monster. Now their task was to free Epos the Winged Flame. Normally, Epos protected the kingdom from the volatile volcano just outside the capital city. But now that it was under Malvel's evil spell, there was no telling what could happen, especially if the volcano were allowed to erupt!

Tom pulled his shield from his back and used it to crush some bracken — dense ferns that would make for a soft place to sit. "Let's rest for a few minutes while we check the map," he said to Elenna.

"Great!" said Elenna, slumping to the ground beside Silver. "I thought we'd never stop."

Storm leaned over and rested his muzzle on her shoulder, snorting softly.

Two leather bags hung down on either side of Storm's saddle, and Tom reached into one to pull out the magical map of Avantia. It had been given to them by the king's closest adviser — the wizard Aduro.

Tom sat beside Elenna. As his finger traced the trees, hills, and lakes, the pictures rose up from the parchment, standing as tall as his thumbnail. A pulsing red line marked the path he and Elenna had taken from the ice fields of the far north to this great forest of the east.

"We're nearly at the forest's edge," said Tom with relief.

Elenna pointed to a mountain on the map, just beyond the forest. "That must be the volcano." As she watched, tiny puffs of smoke rose up from the map's miniature mountain. "I thought the volcano was supposed to be dormant," Elenna said, her brow furrowing.

"Well, it used to be. . . ." Tom thought about this for a moment. If Epos was keeper of the volcano, and if Malvel had put the Winged Flame under a spell, then that meant the volcano might be active. Tom shivered at the thought. The kingdom would be in grave danger if the volcano erupted. A jolt of anticipation ran through him. "Aduro said Epos was the most powerful of all the Beasts."

He frowned at the map. Several villages clustered near the base of the smoking mountain. "Why would anyone build a village that close to a volcano — even a dormant one?"

"The soil around volcanoes is very fertile, so crops grow well," said Elenna. "I learned that from my uncle." She looked down at her hands. "It's been so long since I left my village. I miss the people there."

Tom smiled. "When we finish our Quest, you'll return as a hero."

"But what about you?" said Elenna. "Will you go back to your aunt and uncle?"

"I plan to," said Tom, looking away.

Tom's mother had died when he was born, and his father, Taladon, had disappeared soon afterward. Tom had been raised by his aunt and uncle — but he still hoped to find his father some-day. All he knew was that Taladon had served King Hugo in the past, just as Tom was doing now.

"Wait." Tom's nose twitched. A faint breeze had begun to blow. "Can you smell smoke?"

Elenna sniffed at the air and gave a small cough. "Yes, but it's not a campfire. It smells different, somehow."

Suddenly, a loud rumble sounded through the forest and the ground beneath them shook. Storm neighed and reared up in alarm as Tom and Elenna scrambled to their feet. Tom looked up. Through the leaves he glimpsed clouds of dark smoke choking the sky. They were shot through with thin streaks of fire, like shooting stars.

"The volcano!" Elenna gasped.

"We need to find shelter," Tom said. "Epos must be stirring things up!"

Then Elenna froze. "Look," she stammered, staring straight past Tom.

Over the forest's thick trees, a bubbling gray cloud of ash rose into the sky. As it grew, red-hot stones began to pelt down, scorching the treetops and striking the ground with heavy thuds. Tom instinctively grabbed his shield. It would help keep him and Elenna safe, but it was too small to shelter Silver and Storm.

"Quick, we need to find cover!" Tom yelled.

The ground had begun to shake violently. They looked around for anywhere they could seek protection.

"Under that tree!" Elenna screamed, pointing to a large tree with a canopy of thick branches. "We'll be safe over there!"

As they ran frantically toward the tree, larger

and larger stones began to fall from the sky. The blazing volcanic rocks exploded as they hit Tom's shield, raining embers down upon them, stinging their skin. They ran faster, finally collapsing in a heap at the base of the tree.

Tom looked up warily, hoping that the shelter would keep them safe.

CHAPTER TWO

BURNING SECRETS

Huddled under the tree, Tom and Elenna began to have trouble breathing. The air had become thick with gritty volcanic ash and they could no longer see more than a few feet in front of them. They held their shirts up to their noses and mouths to keep from breathing in the toxic air.

After a few moments of terrible shaking, the ground became still again. Rocks stopped falling, and the thundering rumble was replaced by an eerie quiet.

"Are you okay?" Tom coughed and gasped.

"I think so," Elenna replied with a small quiver. "We need to get out of this forest and see if the village is okay."

Tom nodded his head and began gathering his sword and shield.

Peering through the smoke, Tom was reminded of the heavy ocean fog they encountered when they had fought the second Beast, Sepron the Sea Serpent. Thinking about all they had seen on their Quest — and all they had survived — gave Tom a boost in courage.

"Let's go!" he said, leading his companions out from under the massive tree. It was still hard to see, but the smoke seemed to be lifting.

"Hello?" Tom called out, hoping they were close enough to the village to be heard. "Hello?"

His voice drifted off into the still forest.

They continued walking, picking their

way around all the debris that had fallen from the sky.

After walking for a while, they came to a fork in the trail. As Tom was pulling the map from his bag to see which way they should go, the sound of horse hooves beat in the distance behind them.

Tom and Elenna spun on their heels, turning toward the sound. Storm's ears pricked up and the fur on Silver's back bristled.

"What's that?" Elenna asked.

"It sounds like someone's coming our —" Tom cut his sentence short as a band of masked men appeared through the veil of smoke.

Tom grabbed the hilt of his sword and Silver gave a ferocious growl as the men drew nearer and then came to a halt.

"There's no need for that," called out the largest man. "We are from the village of Stonewin."

Tom loosened his grip on the handle of his sword and breathed a sigh of relief.

"We were on a trading mission in the next village when we heard the eruption," the man continued. "But we must return to make sure everyone in the village is safe."

The man removed his mask to reveal a strong, kind face. He had dark hair and a thick beard. There was concern in his eyes.

"My name is Raymond," he said, "and this is Jacob and Leroy." The other two men took off their masks.

"I'm Tom, and this is Elenna. These are our companions Storm and Silver," Tom said. "We were on our way to your village to help."

Raymond looked Tom up and down, a curious expression on his face. But he didn't question what a boy and girl were doing alone in the dark forest. Instead, he said, "Well, Elenna can ride with me and you can ride your horse. We need to hurry in case the village is in danger."

Elenna climbed on the back of Raymond's steed as Tom mounted Storm. With a whoop, they set off down the forest's trail, racing through the smoke toward the village.

Chapter Three

Escape to the Caves

As they raced along the trail, the thick curtain of smoke parted, and Tom realized they had arrived in the village at the foot of the volcano. A small lava flow was trickling down the side of the steep slope. It was headed right toward the houses at the edge of the village. As the lava flowed, a group of brave villagers were frantically digging a ditch on the hillside to divert the molten rock. Raymond and the other men sprinted up the hill to help.

Without a moment's hesitation, Tom joined the villagers, using his shield to scoop away at the soft soil of the hillside. Every so often he would glance up the volcano's side. Puffs of gray smoke popped from its top as a stream of lava worked its way slowly toward the village.

"We're lucky that wasn't a real eruption," Raymond panted as he heaved piles of dirt with a homemade shovel. "Otherwise the whole village would be buried in lava!"

If what had just occurred was minor, Tom could only imagine what the devastation of a real eruption would be like. He knew that he had to free Epos from the evil spell before something worse happened.

Because the volcanic soil was so soft and fertile, it didn't take long for the villagers to dig a ditch that would channel the lava away from the houses and into the forest. They finished just moments before the molten rock reached the top of the ditch.

As the gurgling molten rock coursed away from the village, Tom stood with the men and watched. Elenna came and joined them. Once they were sure the ditch would divert the lava, they made their way back down the hillside to the village.

"Do you think Epos did this?" Elenna asked Tom in a whisper as they reached a cluster of houses.

Tom nodded slowly, watching the deadly lava snake past the edge of the village and into the forest.

"We have to do something," Tom said. "And quick."

Just then a skinny, fair-haired boy of about Tom's age burst out of the forest, coughing hard, a singed sack in one hand. A collar-shaped piece of old armor protected his chin and neck. He flopped down on the grass near one of the houses.

Elenna and Tom ran over to him.

"Are you all right?" Tom asked the boy, helping him to take off the armor around his neck. "What's your name?"

"Owen," he croaked, staring up at them. Soot covered his face. "Our village is going to be destroyed!"

Elenna gave him some of her water, and the boy drank thirstily. "Don't worry," she reassured him. "The lava isn't going to harm your village."

Owen gasped as he tried to catch his breath.

"She's right," Tom said. "Your village is safe — for now at least." Then, getting a better look at the armor, he grabbed Owen by the shoulder. "Where did you get this?"

Owen frowned. "I . . . I found it in the caves."

"Where's the rest of it?" Tom demanded. He tried to keep his feelings under control, but he could feel his fingers tighten on the boy's shoulder.

"I don't know!" Owen wailed, pulling away. He jumped to his feet and scowled at Tom, rubbing his shoulder.

"Tom!" Elenna dragged his hand away. "What's gotten into you?"

"Sorry," he murmured. "But you see . . . this armor was made at the forge where I grew up." He pointed to a small hammer design stamped into the metal. "My uncle stamped his hallmark on everything he sold."

Elenna took the armor and studied it. "Hey, there's something else scratched here." She rubbed soot and rust away from the plate's metal rim and read, "T . . . A . . . L . . . A . . ."

"Taladon," whispered Tom, his stomach clenching with excitement. "Elenna — this armor belonged to my father!" Tom tried on the piece of armor. It fit perfectly.

Elenna stared at him. "That means your father was a knight?"

"I don't know," Tom admitted.

At least, Tom had never been told his father was a knight. Tom could barely contain his excitement. What if his father really was a knight? Then, another thought occurred to him — a terrible thought. What was his father's armor doing in the cave? What if his father was dead? Tom felt his stomach sink.

This horrible thought was interrupted when, suddenly, the ground beneath them began to shake again and plumes of crimson fire streaked across the sky.

"The volcano!" Owen gasped.

Elenna clutched at her throat. Tom felt it, too. The air was suddenly much hotter. It stung their skin and each breath burned their lungs.

"Take cover!" roared Raymond. Tom and Elenna lifted Owen and carried him to the shelter of a large oak. Storm stood protectively over him, as pumice stone and soot showered down from above. Silver raced around the clearing, helping Raymond shepherd the exhausted villagers to shelter.

They all waited tensely as the vibrations in the ground slowly subsided.

Raymond wiped soot and sweat from his face. "We can't stop the fires the lava flow has started," he panted. "And if the volcano erupts again we won't stand a chance out in the open. We'll have to shelter in the caves and hope for a miracle."

Elenna looked at Tom. "I wonder if we'll find the rest of that armor?"

Tom's heart thudded in his chest. All his life he had been desperate to know more about his father. Now he had found a clue — at the worst possible time. He shook his head. "The Quest comes first."

Raymond pulled a horn from his pocket. "I'll

sound the emergency signal. Everyone in the village knows to gather at the caves when they hear it."

Elenna frowned. "But if the volcano does erupt, the caves might fill with lava!"

"There's nowhere else we can go," said a woman.

"Wait a moment," said Tom, reaching into Storm's saddlebag for the magical map. He unrolled it and looked closely at the caves. A faint red line threaded through them — a path! He rolled up the map again quickly before anyone could see. "I think there's a way through the caves to safety," he announced. "It comes out not far from the royal city."

"It's possible." Raymond nodded slowly. Then he blew into the horn, a low, booming note that Tom guessed would carry for miles.

Tom and Elenna followed Raymond as he led the way through the village. Storm carried Owen and a wounded woman on his back. Sharp volcanic glass and thick soot coated the roads and buildings. A foul stink of rotten eggs hung in the smoky air. Tom guessed the smell came from the sulfur that had spewed up from the volcano's heart. People trudged along in silence. Silver looked all around as he walked, eyes bright and alert, ready to warn them of the tiniest tremble in the ground.

The rest of the villagers had already reached the caves by the time Raymond and Tom's party arrived. There were several men and women, and they were pale, dirty, and exhausted. Three grimy dogs lay panting at their feet, and Silver trotted over to greet them. An older woman was snapping candles into three, ready to light their way. She gave one piece of candle each to Tom and Elenna with a smile.

Tom stared up into the dark mouth of the cave. Once, long ago, his father must have explored these caves. But had Taladon also encountered Epos?

"I'll lead the way," he said, turning to Raymond. "I've got a map, and I'm more rested than you. I can scout out the tunnels to check that we can all get through with the animals."

Raymond smiled. "You have spirit, Tom. Lead on."

As Tom stepped into the cave, the cold soothed his smarting skin. It was a relief to breathe cooler air. But the deeper they went, the staler the air became.

The clatter of everyone's footsteps filled Tom's ears. Elenna walked behind him, leading Owen by the hand, calling out words of encouragement to all those following. When Tom looked around he could see the villagers clutching their candles, each in their own pool of weak light. They looked like ghosts in the inky blackness. Rumbles from the volcano made dirt fall from the dark ceiling.

The dogs began to whine, but Silver gave a stern bark and they fell silent. The wounded woman stirred on Storm's back, half-asleep with exhaustion, as the stallion stepped cautiously through the winding passages.

Tom led the way down slopes and picked his way up treacherous pathways. His eyes ached from peering at the map. Finally, the group reached a fork in the rocky tunnel — and the red line on the parchment faded.

"We must be close to the royal city," said Tom. "But how do we get out?"

Elenna checked the map and frowned. "Looks as though we'll have to find our own way from here."

Tom looked at the passage to his left. "I think there's been a rockfall," he whispered. "Perhaps there was an exit there once — but now it's completely sealed."

Another rumble sounded through the ancient stone. Tom tried to stop the panic rising up inside him. But he had to tell Elenna what he was thinking.

"There's no way out," he said, turning to his friend. "We're trapped!"

Chapter Four

Tales of the Past

"Tom," whispered Elenna, her eyes dark with fear. "If these caves fill with lava, we won't stand a chance. We'll all die!"

Tom swallowed hard. "I know."

"What's wrong?" a woman called nervously.

"Nothing," he said, not wanting the villagers to panic. "I'll just scout ahead. Wait here."

But he had barely walked more than a few steps when he froze. A chill of fear ran through him.

He could hear a scraping noise coming from the pile of rocks in front of them. Something was trying to break through!

"Epos?" Elenna hissed.

Tom gripped his sword, ready for action. "We'll soon find out!"

Then, to Tom's surprise, Silver leaped forward and jumped up at the rocks. He was yelping and whining eagerly. Tom placed his ear against the rock — and felt relief flood his whole body.

"We're here!" he shouted, beating the hilt of his sword on the rocks. "Can you hear me?"

"What are you doing?" Elenna cried, as a hubbub started up among the villagers.

"I heard voices," he explained. "There are people outside. A rescue party!"

Dust showered down on Silver as a huge rock was heaved away. Weak sunlight stole into the dark cave, and a man wearing a helmet stuck his head through the hole. Tom recognized the crest on the helmet at once.

"It's one of King Hugo's soldiers!" he cried.

"We have some survivors, men," the soldier shouted over his shoulder, then he turned back

and looked at the soot-covered people. "I'm here to rescue the villagers from the volcano. Everyone out, quickly — there could be another rockfall at any moment."

Tom stepped aside and watched the villagers as they scrambled out into the daylight. As the soldiers helped them through, he felt a rush of pride. He'd saved them!

"Well done, Tom," said Elenna, smiling as Silver played with three dogs in the wet grass outside. Storm blew softly against her shoulder. "But now I suppose we should head back to the volcano."

Owen heard them as he walked toward the cave's exit. "You're going to try and find that magic bird, aren't you?" he whispered.

Tom frowned. "You know about Epos?"

Elenna put a comforting hand on his shoulder.

"I was lost in the caves," Owen went on. "I think I found her nest. That's where I found your father's armor."

"Where was this nest?" asked Tom.

"I'm not sure," Owen admitted. "I left chalk arrows on the walls to mark where I'd been. But I didn't see any of them on our way here."

"Well, it seems that Epos has a new nest now — in the volcano," Elenna pointed out. "And it could erupt at any moment!"

Suddenly, the king's soldier leaped down into the cave. "What are you two doing?" he asked, peering closely at Tom.

"We have unfinished business in the village," Tom said.

The soldier stared again at Tom's face. "Have I met you before?"

"No, sir," said Tom.

"You remind me of someone I once knew." The soldier nodded. "His name was Taladon."

Elenna gasped, and Tom's eyes widened. "I've heard of Taladon," he said, not wanting to give too much away. "How do you know him?"

The soldier shrugged. "It was many years ago, when King Hugo was new to the throne. He recruited some young knights — and Taladon was one of them."

"He was a knight?" Tom asked, his heart beating faster. "What happened to him?"

The soldier's face fell. "I don't know," he said. He shook Tom's hand, then scrambled back outside.

Tom felt proud and excited. "He knew my father!" His hand tightened around the hilt of his sword. "And my father was a knight! This is my destiny, Elenna. While there's blood in my veins, I will finish the Beast Quest!"

CHAPTER FIVE

THE PLACE OF BATTLE

TOM AND ELENNA CAREFULLY RETRACED THEIR steps through the caves and winding tunnels. Silver went ahead, his tail wagging as he followed the scent back to the village.

"I'm glad we've got him to guide us," said Elenna, peering around in the candlelight. "I don't recognize any of this."

"Me, neither," Tom admitted, leading Storm by his halter. "Hey, what's that?"

Elenna held up her candle to the tunnel wall. A chalk cross had been scratched beside an opening in the rock wall.

"Owen must have left this to mark his way when

he got lost," Tom said. "We could be close to Epos's nest!"

Storm was too large to fit through the gap in the wall. Leaving him to wait in the tunnel, Tom went to see what was on the other side. Elenna and Silver followed him.

They found themselves in a larger cave. By the flickering light of their candles, Tom saw sticks, stones, and dead leaves bundled together in a large, sprawling mess.

"This is definitely a nest," he murmured. Then he saw pieces of silver gleaming in the leaves. With shaking hands, he picked out a piece of leg armor and a chain mail gauntlet. The initial *T* was scratched into each of them.

"Could these be your father's?" Elenna whispered.

Tom nodded. All his life he had longed to know more about his father. Now he felt that his own fate was linked in some strange way to what had happened to him. He put on the leg armor, and pulled the chain mail gauntlet onto his right hand. They fit perfectly.

"Come on, let's get back to Storm," said Elenna.

"There's no time to waste," said Tom grimly. "We've got to stop Epos before the volcano blows wide open!"

Feeling somehow stronger in his father's armor, Tom followed Elenna and Silver back out through the gap in the wall to where Storm was waiting patiently in the dark tunnel. Silver led the way out.

As they emerged from the caves, Tom's heart sank.

The skies were unnaturally dark, as if a terrible storm was about to break. The entire forest seemed ablaze, the treetops lost in a huge cloud of black smoke. A bubbling river of red-hot lava snaked around the base of the volcano, like a moat around a castle.

Tom jumped onto Storm's back and pulled Elenna up behind him. "Come on," he said. "Let's get to the volcano. If I can find Epos and make her angry enough, she'll attack. Then I might just be able to get close enough to break the enchantment."

He pressed his heels to Storm's sides and the stallion leaped forward, galloping through a cluster of singed trees and onto the main road, toward the volcano. Silver had to sprint to keep up, with Elenna calling to him, urging him on.

It became hotter and hotter the closer they got to the volcano. The ground shuddered as they climbed the steep slope, Storm's hooves kicking up ash. The air shimmered with fierce heat. When they neared the base of the volcano, Tom eased Storm to a halt. The stallion hung his head, breathing heavily, his neck and shoulders soaked with sweat.

"Look!" Elenna pointed up at a dark figure

gliding in wide circles above the volcano's summit. "There's Epos!"

Tom felt a thrill of fear and wonder at the sight of the Beast. Its body glowed with a dark, magical light. As he watched, Epos plunged down into the volcano — only to burst back out seconds later in a torrent of flames and boiling lava. The lava seared a burning path down the side of the volcano, slowly pooling into the bubbling moat at the base. The village was now completely covered in the molten rock.

"If Epos keeps stoking the volcano like that, the eruption will be massive," said Tom. "The lava could even reach the royal city."

Elenna looked pale. "King Hugo could end up buried in his own palace!"

"It would leave the whole kingdom in chaos," Tom said gravely. "Exactly what Malvel wants."

"Tom, look!" shouted Elenna, pointing into the sky. "I think Epos has spotted us!"

Tom felt a stab of fear as Epos's screech tore through the smoky air. Grabbing his sword, he locked eyes with the hate-filled Beast. The Winged Flame made a wide circle in the dark sky, slicing through the thick smoke like a lightning bolt. Then, with terrible speed, the giant bird dove straight toward Tom and Elenna!

CHAPTER SIX

THE MOAT OF FIRE

Tom leaped down from Storm, swung his shield from his shoulder, and drew his sword as the shadow of the Beast fell over them. Tom looked up, desperately trying to spot the enchanted collar Malvel had placed on the bird. Epos was moving so quickly it was hard to be sure, but Tom thought he caught a glimpse of a golden glimmer around the bird's neck.

With a battle cry, he lunged upward, his sword held high above his head. If he could just grab the enchanted band . . .

But Epos's deadly talons knocked the blade from

· 45 ·

his hand and sent it flying through the air. Storm reared up and kicked the air as the flame bird swept overhead, sparks of fire peppering the air in her wake. Silver barked ferociously, baring his teeth.

In panic, Tom looked around for his sword. It must have fallen in the bushes behind him. He would never find it in time to defend against another attack!

But then he saw what Elenna was doing. She had climbed down from Storm and pulled her bow from one of his saddlebags. Then she raised her weapon and took careful aim.

Whoosh! As Epos swooped down, Elenna shot an arrow. The Beast screeched and turned nimbly to avoid it. Quickly, Elenna sent another arrow after the first. It whistled past the creature's head. The Beast's eyes burned crimson with rage, then she turned and soared away, spiraling up through the thick smoke toward the mouth of the volcano.

"Elenna, you did it!" Tom yelled. "You drove her away!"

Silver barked behind them. He had pulled Tom's sword from the bushes with his teeth. Tom patted the wolf and picked up his weapon.

"How are we ever going to cross that lava to climb the volcano?" Elenna wondered.

"*We're* not," said Tom. "But I am."

She frowned. "Alone?"

He picked up his shield. "This protects me from fire — and after the battle with Tagus the Night Horse, it can also help me reach amazing speeds. I can use it as a raft and skim across the surface of the lava."

Elenna's frown deepened. "But, Tom, if you fall in —"

"There's no other way," Tom insisted. "And

there's no room to take anyone else. I'll stand my best chance of defeating Epos in the heart of her territory, at the top of the volcano. But she might try to attack me as I climb. If she does, I'll need you to drive her off again with those arrows."

"I won't let you down." Elenna's eyes narrowed with determination.

Fear, excitement, and anticipation were all jumbled up inside Tom. But he knew one thing for sure — the greatest trial of his life was approaching.

He hugged Elenna. Storm pushed Tom's arm with his nose, then blew gently on his hair. Tom smiled and stroked his horse's neck. Then he crouched down to say good-bye to Silver. The sleek gray wolf licked his hand and gazed up at him intently.

Tom looked at his friends with a mixture of pride and sorrow. They had all grown so close on their Quest. But now he had to leave them. He turned away and walked down the hillside to the lava's edge. His heart was pounding and his skin prickled with the heat as he carefully slid his shield onto the surface of the molten moat. The enchanted wood hissed and steamed.

"Here goes," said Tom, holding his breath as he stepped lightly onto the shield. It wobbled, but held firm beneath him. Then he dug his sword against the bank and pushed with all his might, propelling himself across the moat of lava.

White-hot drops of lava spat up from the seething lake of fire, and Tom held his arms out to help him balance as his shield skated across the surface, picking up speed as it went. The dragon scale given to him by Ferno and the horseshoe from Tagus were both helping him to cross the deadly moat!

As Tom reached the other side, he jumped for solid ground with a whoop of joy. He had made it!

He heard Elenna cheering, and waved to her.

But as he pulled his shield out of the lava, the ground shook beneath his feet. He looked up to see Epos still circling through the fire-clouds that belched from the top of the volcano.

Up there, his destiny was waiting.

Tom slung the shield over his shoulder, slipped his sword into its scabbard, and started to climb.

→ Chapter Seven ←

The Dark Figure

Tom scaled huge crags of rock, making his way toward the summit of the volcano. But the ground grew more and more treacherous. Several times he slipped on loose stones and almost fell. He was clinging to a sheer rock face when Epos caught sight of him through the black clouds. With a piercing shriek, the Beast swooped down to attack.

Tom went for his shield. But Epos grabbed hold of it with her beak and wrenched it out of Tom's hands.

"No!" Tom shouted, panic-stricken. He yanked his sword from his scabbard and swung wildly at

Epos. The Beast retreated a little way, still holding the shield in her beak, just out of Tom's reach. Then she turned and flew away, fire streaming in her wake.

Tom felt sick as he wiped sweat from his brow. He had lost his best defense — his magical shield. But he had come too far to turn back now.

He continued his steep climb. Stinking smoke gushed from vents in the trembling rock, stinging his eyes. His throat and lungs burned every time he breathed in, and the fumes made him light-headed. Tom stopped for a moment and drank thirstily from his water bottle. Battling Epos on this terrain wasn't going to be easy — if he didn't stumble off the path in all this smoke and fall to his doom first.

"Turn back, Tom. This Quest is beyond you now."

The icy whisper came from behind him. Tom whirled around in surprise.

A tall figure in dark robes was standing just a few paces away, wreathed in sickly yellow smoke. Its face was hidden by a hood. Its thin arms were folded across its chest. The figure made Tom shiver, despite the fierce heat.

"Who . . . who are you?" Tom stammered.

"You know who I am." The figure took a step toward him. "I am Malvel."

Tom felt a dizzying rush of terror. The Dark Wizard, who had enslaved all the Beasts of Avantia for his own evil purpose, was standing before him! With trembling hands, Tom tightened his grip on his sword.

Malvel laughed. "I know you're brave, Tom, but I didn't think you were stupid. Do you really think a sword can harm me?"

"Stay back," said Tom, trying to stop his voice from shaking.

"You and Aduro are both fools," rasped the dark, hooded figure. "While he has been watching you trek through the kingdom freeing the Beasts, he's been too distracted to hunt for me — and Epos, the most powerful Beast of all." Malvel strode away through the smoke. "You have served me well, boy. Just like your father . . ."

Tom felt a shiver run through him. "You don't know my father. You're lying."

"Taladon helped me a great deal," said Malvel. "My plans could not have succeeded without him."

"Liar!" Tom bellowed. He raised his sword and angrily flung himself at the hooded figure.

With a laugh of triumph, Malvel disappeared.

Chapter Eight

THE WILL TO SURVIVE

Tom stood on the lip of the volcano feeling lost and powerless. Had Malvel really used his father? The thought seemed too terrible to even consider. For a brief moment, Tom forgot about everything he had been through. He had come so close to finishing his Quest, but now he was not sure he could. If his father couldn't succeed, how could he?

Before Tom had a chance to feel any worse, he caught a glimpse of Epos out of the corner of his eye. The Winged Flame was coming to finish him off!

No! thought Tom fiercely. *I won't let my Quest end this way.* He hadn't set free the first five Beasts only to be beaten by the last! He thought of the way Malvel had tricked and almost killed him — and an angry determination built up inside him. He would fight Malvel and his evil plans to his last breath. Tom was still clutching his sword, and now he gripped it more tightly than ever.

"I'll never stop fighting," he gasped.

With a burst of energy, Tom jumped for the golden band around Epos's neck as the Winged Flame swooped by. But he couldn't quite reach it. He stretched and strained, but it was no use.

Epos circled back, gaining more speed as she dove through the smoky sky. Once more Tom reached up to cut the golden band — just as Epos changed direction. The sword slipped from his grip and tumbled down into the volcano.

"No!" yelled Tom. He felt numb. He had lost

his shield and his sword. How could he ever win now?

I've still got my wits, he thought bravely. "I'm not giving up!" he yelled at Epos.

As if Epos had understood him, she circled back toward Tom, swooping low. This was his chance! Before the Beast could knock him into the fiery crater, Tom twisted around and grabbed hold of her leg. It was like holding a burning log. Tom shouted in pain but he couldn't stop now.

Epos gave a bellow of rage and tried to shake Tom free. The lava bubbled greedily below them.

"I won't let go!" Tom shouted.

But now Epos was flying toward the volcano's rim. Tom realized she was planning to break his grip by smashing him against the face of the rock! It loomed closer and closer.

At the last moment, Tom let go of Epos and twisted through the air. He seemed to fall for

ages — but at last he landed on a narrow ledge, the impact jarring his whole body as he scrambled for a handhold. The rock was burning hot and scorched his skin. But, with the last of his strength, he managed to cling on.

Epos was still circling above him, screeching in fury, and Tom knew he didn't have a hope of climbing over the edge of the rim. *I'm trapped*, he thought. *An easy target*. But then he saw a crack in the rock — a long, smoldering split. Was it wide enough for him to fit through? His arms and legs ached, and his skin felt so raw that every movement was agony. But somehow, Tom started to squeeze through the gap. If he was fast enough, Epos might think he had simply fallen to his death, and give up on him.

All I need is a chance to get my strength back, he told himself, *to work out a plan. . . .*

With a last, exhausting effort, Tom wriggled

through the split in the stone and fell a short way onto another, cooler ledge — outside the volcano and out of the great flame bird's reach.

Tom lay on the shuddering, smoking ground, gasping for breath. He was overlooking a small, rocky plain close to the volcano's summit. He had no weapons and nowhere to take cover. A dark, steep slope towered above him, leading back up to the mouth of the volcano.

Tom realized then that the crack he had squeezed through was part of a thick black split running horizontally across the slope.

A desperate hope flared up inside him. Above that split were balanced thousands of tons of rock — which seemed to be leaning back into the volcano. If only there was some way of bringing it crashing down, it might plug the fiery heart of the volcano — and ruin Malvel's plans.

"You are too late, boy," came an icy whisper. "Your Quest ends here."

Tom spun around to find that the sinis

hooded figure of Malvel had reappeared on the

plain in front of him.

Then Epos came swooping down from the rim

of the volcano. Tom saw two red eyes glaring down

at him. The Beast's giant beak snapped open. Her

dark, glowing wings unfolded, and her talons

glinted in the dim, crimson light.

The flame bird lunged forward, ready to tear

Tom to pieces.

CHAPTER NINE

THE FIRES OF DESTRUCTION

WITH A GRUNT OF EFFORT, TOM THREW himself out of Epos's path. The Beast was going too fast to stop and crashed into the rock face. Tom scrambled back up.

Tom tried to escape from the ledge. But Epos was too fast. She lashed out with one wing and caught Tom on the back of the neck. Tom gasped as he was knocked forward, landing with a thud. Before he could rise, Epos grabbed him with her enormous beak. Tom shouted out with pain — it was like being gripped in a vice. Then the Winged Flame flung him to the ground. Every muscle ached. His body burned with bruises.

But still he forced himself back to his feet.

Tom stared as Epos hovered above him. Even in his fear, he found the giant flame bird a breathtaking sight.

Suddenly, Epos dropped down and grabbed Tom's chest in her huge talons.

Tom cried out in pain as the giant Winged Flame began to squeeze, crushing his ribs.

"Look at the great young hero," Malvel sneered. "You are as weak as your father."

"You're not fit to speak of my father," Tom gasped. He wrestled with Epos's claws, trying to weaken the Beast's grip. The pain was incredible, and the world was starting to spin. "I believe in him," he said through gritted teeth, "as I believe in the Beasts' right to be free!"

Epos's grip on Tom grew tighter still. The ground groaned and shook as the volcano prepared to explode.

"And I believe," Tom croaked, clutching

desperately at the Beast's leg, "that it's my destiny . . . to beat YOU!"

Tom's right hand — the one on which he wore his father's chain mail gauntlet — closed on the locked golden band around Epos's neck.

To Tom's amazement, it tore through the band as if it were wet paper. He stared at the scraps of gold in his hand.

Epos let go of Tom and shrieked. It was a noise like the earth's core cracking open. She shook violently, thrashing her wings, then rose up gracefully into the air, released at last.

"No!" bellowed Malvel, backing away. "It is not possible!"

Then Epos flew straight at Malvel, grabbing him with her lethal talons and lifting him up above the volcano.

"This is not the end, Tom!" Malvel screamed. "We shall meet again!"

Epos held the dark, struggling figure above the flames exploding from the mouth of the volcano.

Then the Dark Wizard disappeared in a haze of white light, and the Beast's talons were left clutching empty air. Had Malvel's dark magic destroyed him? Or had he somehow transported himself to safety? Tom didn't know.

With a rasping shriek, Epos plunged down inside the volcano. Tom heard the echoes of the shriek hang in the air for a few moments. Then they too were gone.

"I've done it," Tom murmured. His body was burned and bleeding, but he couldn't stop smiling. "Whatever has happened to Malvel, his plans have been defeated — because I've set Epos free!"

Just then the ground bucked beneath him, and a split opened up, belching fire and thick yellow smoke. Tom sat up in sudden terror. This was no time to congratulate himself. The volcano was about to blow. The kingdom of Avantia was still in danger!

Panting for breath, Tom stared at the steep slope of rock shielding him from the fiery force of the volcano. So many cracks were running across it, and he remembered his desperate plan. If he could topple all that rock, it just might plug the volcano!

Tom yanked off his father's leg armor. Each piece had a pointed end. He placed one end against a narrow crack and grabbed a rock to use as a hammer. He just had to drive the spikes into the cracks to widen the splits. With luck it might bring the rock face tumbling down.

Choking on smoke, he struck the pointed armor again and again. The cracks started to widen — but the rock face didn't move. Desperately, Tom scooped up the other piece of armor and wedged it into another crack.

I can do this, he told himself, swinging his rock hammer again and again. Tears of frustration welled up in his eyes. The piece of rock slipped from his numb fingers.

It was no good. Tom simply wasn't strong enough.

Suddenly, he felt something watching him. He spun around.

Epos was hovering in the sky above. The Beast's eyes were no longer red. They shone like the purest gold.

As Tom stared in amazement, the Beast flew down and crashed into the rock. Again and again, Epos hurled herself at the stone. Huge splits opened up in the rock as Epos drove her beak into the stone.

"You understand!" Tom cried in amazement. "You saw what I was trying to do, and you're helping me!" He felt torn. He was so grateful for the Beast's help, but it was awful to watch her flinging herself against the rocks, violet sparks flying from her body.

With new hope, Tom grabbed another lump of stone and used it to drive his crumpled leg armor deeper still inside the cracks. Working together, he and Epos might just succeed.

At last, the huge slope of rock began to crumble! Black zigzags were spreading across it.

"Yes!" Tom cried.

With a last, roaring shriek, Epos flung herself into the center of the rock face. With a grating, grinding noise, it collapsed.

Tom was standing at the edge of the slope, but the giant bird had no time to get clear.

"Epos!" Tom yelled as the Beast disappeared beneath the falling rocks and into the mouth of the volcano.

CHAPTER TEN

THE FINAL ANSWERS

Tom was knocked to his knees as the ground rocked beneath him. He covered his ears as huge crashes echoed all around.

Then the tremors died away. Smoke, mixed with dust, rose up into the black sky. For a long, stunned moment, Tom wondered why it was suddenly so much darker. Then he realized that the fierce glow of the molten lava had been buried beneath thousands of tons of rock. The volcano's fires had been put out.

The kingdom was safe at last!

But Epos was dead. The noble Beast had sacrificed herself for the sake of Avantia.

"No!" Tom shouted, scrambling over the fallen rock, trying to find some way of reaching the flame bird. But there was no way through.

Tom barely noticed when some of the swirling smoke began to shine and sparkle, and a familiar, red-cloaked shape appeared beside him. At last he turned.

"Hello, Wizard Aduro," Tom whispered.

The old man smiled down at him. "You have done well, Tom. You have defeated Malvel — and saved the kingdom."

Tom cast a glance at the base of the volcano where the village used to stand. The lava had begun to cool, turning a dark red. The forest fires had burned themselves out, and each tree was now a black skeleton. "I still don't understand how I broke the band to set Epos free," he admitted, removing the chain mail gauntlet and drawing out the wizard's key from around his neck. "I didn't even need the enchanted key."

Aduro smiled. "It was your faith in your father and your friends — and your faith in yourself — that allowed you to break the evil charm. Malvel did not understand goodness or loyalty. So his charms had no defense against one who prized those things so highly."

Tom's gaze fell to the ground. "But I couldn't save Epos. She's dead."

"Are you sure?" the old wizard said gently.

A deep rumbling sound rolled around them. Before Tom could react, an enormous ball of light rose up from the sealed volcano. Something stirred inside it — the golden shadow of a bird. Then the ball of light burst apart and, with a mighty squawk, a gigantic, majestic creature appeared.

"Epos!" Tom cried.

"She is a phoenix," Wizard Aduro reminded him. "She must allow herself to die in flames, so that she can rise anew from the ashes."

The Beast circled above them, flapping her golden wings, leaving trails of golden fire in the air.

"Now that she has thrown off her old form, all trace of Malvel's evil has died with it," Aduro murmured. "Thanks to you, Tom, she will be free forever."

"Wait," whispered Tom. "There's something in her mouth. . . ."

Epos opened her beak. A smoking sword and a blackened, wooden disc fell out, landing with a clatter at Tom's feet.

"My sword! My shield!" Tom shouted. "Epos brought them back from the volcano!"

With a last, deafening screech, Epos soared up into the heavens. In her wake she left streaks of magical fire that burned away the dark clouds of volcanic smoke and ash hanging over the village.

Tom laughed as he found himself staring up into the clear blue sky of an early morning.

Aduro put a hand on Tom's shoulder. "It is a new dawn for the whole kingdom — thanks to you, Tom."

Just then, something else fell from the sky, right into Tom's hand. It was a golden feather, still blazing with the phoenix's heat. Instinctively, Tom knelt to place it in his shield. At once, a golden light shone out from the shield and bathed his skin.

"Aduro?" Tom called uncertainly. "Where are you?"

"Do not be afraid," the wizard murmured. "Someone special wishes to see you — and he does not like to be kept waiting. . . ."

Tom felt a jolt go through his body. His senses spun. He felt as if he were flying. Then the air was suddenly fresh and sweet in his lungs. All was quiet. Gingerly, he opened his eyes to find himself in a large, luxurious room, decorated in crimson and gold. He was kneeling on a polished floor of white marble. A man sat in front of him on a magnificent throne.

With a gasp, Tom realized where he was. He was in the royal palace with his sword and shield — on his knees before the king!

"Greetings, Tom," said King Hugo. "Wizard Aduro has brought you directly to me so I can thank you without delay."

Tom gulped and bowed his head. "It was my pleasure, Your Majesty!"

"All Avantia owes you a great debt," the king went on. "Ask for anything you desire, and you shall have it."

Tom rose to his feet and bowed. "Please, Your Majesty, all I want is the answer to one question. . . ." He swallowed hard. "What happened to my father?"

"It is time you knew," the king said. "Taladon the Swift was a young knight. Many years ago he encountered Epos in the caves near the volcano.

Epos was under no spell, but she thought your father was an intruder. Your father fought the Beast — and lost. And from that day on, he made it his mission to know all he could about the Beasts. He went to stay with his brother in Errinel, read old books, gathered secret knowledge . . . and found a wife, of course."

Tom nodded. "My mother."

"Soon after, Taladon began to dream about the Beasts. Strange and awful nightmares which told him that something bad was going to happen. These nightmares did not go away. . . ." King Hugo leaned forward. "He believed they were a prophecy that would one day come true. So did your mother. And because they both loved you, they wanted to protect the land in which you would grow up."

Tom listened, astounded, as the king went on.

"Your mother's dying wish was that Taladon should go on a Quest to find out more about the

Beasts. That he should track them down all over the world, learn their strengths and weaknesses. That way, if they ever did attack, the kingdom would be prepared — and its people could live without fear."

"But, Your Majesty," Tom began nervously, "Malvel said my father helped him."

Wizard Aduro stepped up beside him. "Malvel stole Taladon's journals, filled with hard-won secret knowledge of the Beasts," he explained. "He used that information to gain control over six of them. That is the only way in which your father helped Malvel."

Tom felt a surge of pride in his father's achievements. "Then I have followed in his footsteps!" He looked hopefully at Aduro. "Do you know where he is now?"

"I do not," Aduro admitted. "He has traveled to faraway lands now, to places even I cannot see."

"One day I'll find him," Tom vowed. "We will meet, I know it. It's my destiny."

Suddenly, there was a clattering noise outside the throne room, and voices raised in surprise.

The king smiled. "Ah! Aduro has conjured some others who wish to greet you."

The doors to the throne room were thrown open — by Elenna!

"Tom!" she yelled.

Before Tom could say a word, Elenna threw herself into his arms, almost knocking him to the floor as she hugged him tight. "Oh, Tom, you did it!"

"*We* did it," he told her. "I could never have done this without you, Storm, and Silver. Where are they?"

"It seems they are inside my throne room!" King Hugo exclaimed.

Tom laughed as Storm clopped over and pushed

past Aduro, neighing loudly. Silver dashed in and out of the stallion's legs in excitement, then licked Tom all over his face.

"I'm not sure I've ever entertained a horse and a wolf in my palace before," laughed King Hugo. "But then, we've never had a hero like Tom before, either." He beamed at Elenna and the animals. "Tonight there shall be a mighty feast — with you, Tom, and Elenna as the guests of honor!"

Tom bowed. "We are grateful, Your Majesty," he said.

"I am the grateful one," said King Hugo. "I shall speak to the people now."

As the king crossed to the royal balcony, Tom looked at Aduro. "Is it really all over? Is Malvel gone forever?"

"Who can tell?" said Aduro. "Malvel was a great sorcerer with the power to travel great distances in the blink of an eye. This Quest may be over, Tom, but others may lie ahead."

A shiver of excitement ran through Tom. "I'll be ready."

"And we'll face them together," said Elenna.

Storm whinnied and Silver barked, as a gigantic cheer shook the palace. King Hugo had walked out onto the balcony to greet the people of Avantia, and now he was beckoning to Tom and Elenna.

Tom gulped. "We'd better go and face that crowd!"

Tom and Elenna took their place at King Hugo's side. The streets outside were jammed full of jostling people, all of them clapping and cheering. Tom spotted Owen and Raymond smiling in the crowd, and waved to them.

"You're the kingdom's hero, Tom!" said Elenna excitedly. "Your story will be told throughout the land. . . ."

Tom hardly heard her. For a second he thought he glimpsed a dark, hooded figure. . . . He blinked — and when he looked again, there was nothing. Were his eyes playing tricks on him?

If Malvel returns, Tom thought gravely, *I shall be waiting*.

But right now, it was enough to know that he had completed his Beast Quest, and that Elenna, Storm, and Silver were close beside him.

Tom smiled and held his sword aloft as the crowd cheered. He thought about the six Beasts, who were now free again to guard the kingdom. Just as they always had, since time began.

Out of the darkness, a hero will rise.

THE SECRETS OF DROON

By Tony Abbott

Under the stairs, a magical world awaits you!

Read all of my
FABUMOUSE
ADVENTURES!